The Exiled Prince

The Exiled Prince

The Story of Daniel From
Captive Lad to Prime
Minister of the World
Empires

By

Elizabeth Rice Handford

SWORD of the LORD
PUBLISHERS
P.O. BOX 1099, MURFREESBORO, TN 37133

Copyright 1971 by
Sword of the Lord Publishers

ISBN 0-87398-208-8

Library of Congress
Catalog Card Number:
73-189664

Printed and bound in the United States of America

TABLE OF CONTENTS

Chapter   Page

1. Surrender or Die!

The first shafts of sunlight crept up over the great city walls of Jerusalem, revealing a young boy slumped across a stone battlement. Weariness had drained his body, but his dark eyes darted back and forth across the valley, piercing the gloom to watch every movement of the enemy.

He was a young lad—but he held his bow and arrow at the ready, like a true soldier of Judah.

It was the year 607 before Christ. Nebuchadnezzar, the new king of Babylon, had surrounded Jerusalem. His army covered the hills like grasshoppers. It was terrifying to see those unending columns of soldiers riding forward on their fierce horses, their tall spears glinting gold in the early sunlight.[1] The siege had lasted for many days, for the walls of Jerusalem were thick and high and strong. But the gates of the city were wood. If Nebuchadnezzar's soldiers ever got past the arrows of the men on the wall, the city was doomed. And Nebuchadnezzar's army was already famous for its cruelty and mercilessness.[2]

The lad Daniel was depressed. His throat ached

from burden. How long could they hold back that terrible army? How long could they fight without any food to eat? City gates, if they were barred to keep out the enemy, could not be opened to bring food in. People were starving. Dead bodies already lay in the streets, and no one had strength to bury them. Soon the soldiers would not be able to fight. Then that wicked army would storm into the helpless city, stabbing, spearing, looting and burning. And there wasn't a thing Daniel could do to help! He wiped a tear from his face, and kept watching.

As daylight broadened, men in the Babylonian camp below stirred. Daniel heard a pebble drop, and he whirled sharply.

"It's me, Hananiah, Daniel. I'm coming up," a voice whispered in the darkness below, inside the wall.

"Watch it, Hananiah. There's an archer over there using this position for his target practice! Keep low."

"I will," Hananiah answered. Breathing hard, he crept up beside Daniel. He looked through the embrasure, and saw the thousands of soldiers moved into position to attack. He whistled in dismay. "The world is filled with Babylonian soldiers!"

"Almost," Daniel agreed.

"I wish we could fight them, instead of holing up in the city like this. We could rush them at night, kill them all before they knew what was happening. Or, better yet, we could get them confused, and let them kill each other like Gideon's men did.[3] If Gideon could do it, with only 300 soldiers, so could we." He stopped to take a breath.

"God was with Gideon," Daniel said sadly. "God isn't with us."

Hananiah hung his head. It was true. God had forsaken them. But it wasn't God's fault. They had forsaken God. Even now, at dawn, you could still smell the horrible stench from the Valley of Hinnom, though it was on the other side of the city. Last night, like so many other nights, the leaders of Jerusalem had bowed down to the heathen idol Molech. They had heated it white-hot, and then thrown a screaming baby to death in its blistering arms. People who had once worshipped God sacrificed a human being to a wicked idol! No wonder God had forsaken Judah!

Hananiah shook his head. "If only King Jehoiakim would turn back to God!"[5]

"Jeremiah the prophet keeps trying to reach him—he just won't give up."

"Suppose the King of Egypt would come and fight for us?"

"Not a chance," Daniel answered. "Nebuchadnezzar has conquered every bit of land from the Euphrates River to the Nile. There'll be no help from the Pharaoh!"[6]

"Oh, what's the use?" Hananiah burst out. "We

may as well die by that soldier's arrow as to stay in this rotting city!"

"No, Hananiah, don't say that. God will do right. I know He will. I've made up my mind to trust Him no matter which way things go. I'm going to keep praying and keep fighting."

Hananiah looked at Daniel scornfully. "You're just a kid, Daniel. What can you do? If the grown-ups are all cowards—" Hananiah stopped abruptly, ashamed at the burning look in Daniel's eyes. "But when I think about it," he mumbled, "I guess if God was going to listen to anybody pray, it would be you. Nobody else around here seems to love Him at all."

"In fact, they blame God for the war, don't they? No matter, Hananiah, *we* can do right. *We* can serve God. You'll see."

A low whistle made the boys turn around. "Azariah! Careful as you come!" Daniel called to the friend scrambling up the wall.

Azariah ducked as an arrow sang over his head. "Daniel, you and Hananiah are wanted at once in the courtyard of the temple."

"Us? Who would want us, and what for?"

Azariah's face was white. "The king has surrendered to King Nebuchadnezzar."

"Surrendered?" Hananiah wailed. "We'll all be killed!"

"No, King Nebuchadnezzar has promised mercy to all."

Daniel nodded thoughtfully. "That could be true. Don't you remember the Prophet Jeremiah kept telling the king God wanted him to surrender?" [7]

Hananiah brightened. "I do remember now."

"What are the conditions of the surrender, Azariah? Do you know?"

"Yes. He wants a certain number of hostages to take back to Babylon. The list is already made up."

"Hostage? What's a hostage?" Hananiah asked.

"People he'll take back to Babylon to make sure King Jehoiakim does what he promises. If King Jehoiakim breaks his promise—" Azariah drew his finger across his throat," then the hostages will lose their heads."

"Who will be the hostages?" Hananiah asked soberly.

Azariah's voice trembled. "The sons of the princes. Your name is on the list. Mine. Daniel. And Mishael."

"You mean we've got to be held prisoners in Babylon because King Jehoiakim surrendered?" Hananiah asked.

Azariah nodded, unable to speak.

"All the way to Babylon?"

Azariah nodded.

Daniel laid down his bow and arrows reluctantly.

"I've prayed, so many times, for the end of this war, and now that it's here, I'm scared to death."

"Me, too." Hananiah echoed.

"But if this is what God wants, then I want it, too," Daniel spoke softly.

"You must come now. They are waiting for us in the temple courtyard."

Hurriedly, their hearts pounding with fear, the three boys scrambled down the wall, and raced toward the temple. Captives in Babylon! How would it be? Would they die there? Or would wicked King Jehoiakim for once in his life keep a promise? Would they ever see their fathers and mothers again? Did God truly care what was happening to them?

2. In Sight of the Blue Enamelled Walls of Babylon

The temple courtyard was a jumble of confusion. The great olivewood doors, once overlaid with gold, were now gouged where soldiers' knives had pried it away. Judean soldiers hurried out with the beautiful gold vessels King David had made many years before, and dedicated to God.⁸ The women and children stood around the edges of the milling crowd, their thin faces marked with fear.

"Where do we go, Azariah?" Daniel asked.

"Over there, by that pillar."

"Can we see our folks before we leave?"

"Who knows? King Nebuchadnezzar said the truce is off if King Jehoiakim isn't ready by noon, with the hostages, and vessels of gold from the temple."

The three youths hurried to the appointed place. Daniel's friend, Mishael, was already there. He squeezed Daniel's hand nervously. Some of the lads were trembling, too frightened to think of hiding their fears.

A trumpet blast cut through the noise. Everyone hushed. The captain of the host stepped onto the porch of the temple. "His Royal Highness, Jehoiakim, King of Judah!"

Everyone dropped to his knees. Jehoiakim stepped out on the porch. Daniel had not seen the king for many days. He was shocked at the king's appearance. His eyes were bloodshot. His beard was tangled and dirty. The king's lips curled in a sneer. "I thank my most loyal subjects," he said sarcastically, "for your fearless fighting in my behalf. If you were but half men, you could have fought this heathen king, and driven him to his knees."

Daniel gasped. Azariah reached over and covered his mouth in anxiety, lest the soldiers hear. Daniel shoved it away, and whispered, "But we did fight, Azariah! We fought bravely, and many of our men died, still standing in their places!"

"He always finds somebody to blame for his troubles, doesn't he?" Hananiah said hotly.

The king's voice rasped on. "Thanks to you, this day I have lost my throne, and become a vassal to King Nebuchadnezzar. Say good bye, my dear, loyal subjects, to your gold and to your children."

Suddenly a tall, bony-thin man climbed up onto the porch beside King Jehoiakim. It was Jeremiah, the prophet! His face was twisted with grief, and tears streamed down his beard. He fell on his knees before the king, and held out his hands to him. His voice carried to the farthest corner of the courtyard, and the people listened wordlessly as he pleaded with the king. "Ever since Josiah was king," Jeremiah cried, "the word of the Lord has come to me, and I have spoken to you, rising early and speaking, but you wouldn't listen. You haven't listened to any of the other prophets, either. But God promised if you'd turn from your sin, turn away from your idols, you could keep your kingdom. But you wouldn't do it, and now God has given up. King Nebuchadnezzar will ruin this land. He'll make Jerusalem a pile of stones. Our captivity must last for seventy years!" [9]

King Jehoiakim's face turned red with rage. Under his breath, so the crowd could not hear, he hissed, "Jeremiah, I'll have your blood yet! You wait! I killed that prophet Urijah because he didn't know when to keep his mouth shut.[10] I'll get you yet. You wait! Guards, take him away!"

Daniel watched, his stomach churning with disgust, as the soldiers dragged Jeremiah away. "Oh, King Jehoiakim, why don't you repent? Are you going to ruin the land forever?. . .Dear Lord, please help him be sorry. Please don't let it be too late!"

But it was too late. God had given him up!

The events of the surrender were a confused blur in

Daniel's memory: the long march from the temple out through the city gate, past the lines of Babylonian soldiers: the dazzling sight of the King of Babylon dressed in gold; the abject humility of King Jehoiakim as he promised to obey Nebuchadnezzar; the counting out of the hostages that would go to Babylon to guarantee Jehoiakim's pledge; the sad goodbye to his mother and father.

The long desert march toward Babylon was a nightmare of haste and weariness. The soldiers were cruel. They were hardened to the heat of the sun, the sudden sandstorms that filled the throat, the long hours of riding. But the hostages were young. They had been fighting for months. And they were nearly starved. It was hard to please the wild, untamed soldiers. Daniel worked hard at learning the strange, guttural language of his guards, so he could obey them quickly, and protect the other youths from their anger.

Now, after many days' journey by camel and ass, they were in sight of the great city walls of Babylon. At first it was only a smudge on the horizon. As they rode closer, they could see the broad walls of enamelled gold and blue bricks, topped with beautiful green palm trees.

"It's beautiful!" Mishael gasped.

"Am I glad to see that!" Azariah said.

Daniel smiled ruefully. "Me, too, and that's strange, because I never thought I'd be glad to see Babylon, of all places!"

Hananiah's face clouded. "I'm scared, Daniel, scared to death."

Daniel put his arm around his friend's shoulder. "Me, too, Hananiah. But don't forget, God's been with us so far. He won't fail us now."

"But those soldiers look at us like they'd like to chop our heads off, if only the captains weren't looking."

Azariah kicked at a rock. "There isn't a soul in the world that cares what happens to us."

"No, no, Azariah. You're wrong," Daniel protested. "God cares. And He is as strong out here in the desert as He is in His temple in Jerusalem. Come on. Cheer up. We're still alive. And that's more than we expected three months ago!"

But Daniel's friends found it hard to cheer up. Instead, their footsteps dragged as they got closer and closer to the city. What awful fate awaited them inside those towering walls?

Gateway into Nebuchadnezzar's Palace

3. The First Test

The Babylonian soldiers hastened their captives across the deep, water-filled moat, then through the massive brick walls. The striplings forgot to be frightened as they stared at the magnificent buildings they saw. They were hurried down the broad Avenue of Victory, straight to the King's palace. To their surprise, they were not thrown into a dungeon. Instead, they were taken to a lovely group of rooms at the rear of the palace. They were given basins of water to wash in, and changes of clothing. Then they were brought into a carpeted room, and seated on cushions. A swarthy, blackhaired man waited silently for them, his arms folded across his chest. The whispering of the captives stopped.

"I am Ashpenaz, prince of the eunuchs of my lord King Nebuchadnezzar."

The man spoke Hebrew! Why hadn't they guessed? His dark eyes had watched their every movement throughout the long trip across the desert. Now, they realized he had also understood every word they had said to each other! *Everything* they had said! They had no secrets hidden from him!

"You are surprised I speak Hebrew?" Ashpenaz smiled faintly, his eyebrows arched. "We Babylonians love knowledge of all kinds. That is why my lord, the King of Babylon, instructed me to bring you to this land. I have chosen you for your royal blood, your fair faces, and your bright minds. We will teach you all the wisdom of the Babylonians—the secrets we have learned through a thousand years of study and learning, and watching the movements of the stars. These you will learn. At the end of three years, you will be taken before the King, for his approval.[11]

"You are not to be ordinary slaves. Not, if you stay obedient. But you must not show any of that rebellious spirit for which the kings of Judah are famous. I warn you that King Nebuchadnezzar is terrible in his wrath."

A ghost of a smile crossed Ashpenaz's face. "Now, before you dine, I will give you Babylonian names. I cannot curl my tongue easily around your queer Jewish names."

He walked down the row of boys, assigning a new name to each. For the first time since the boys had left Jerusalem, they laughed out loud. Hebrew names hard to pronounce? Why, those Babylonian names would twist a tongue in two! Hananiah's name was changed to Shadrach. Mishael's new name was Meshach. Azariah became Abed-nego.

When Ashpenaz came to Daniel, he put his arm around his shoulder. Daniel trembled, but stood as tall as he could, and looked straight into the prince's face. Ashpenaz's face softened. "You are a good lad. I have watched you these weeks. You control your mind as well as your body. You have been gentle with these companions, and kind. Yet you were not afraid to fight, were you? Now you face a different kind of fight, but I see, by your eyes, that already you gird for it. You will win this fight, too, I vow. Your name is Daniel. It means, 'God is my judge.' I name you Belteshazzar. An inner voice tells me you shall indeed protect my lord, the king."

Ashpenaz clapped his hands. Servants swarmed into the room, carrying flagons of wine, and platters heaped high with rich foods. "Young men, you may eat. Here is meat and drink sent from the king's table for your pleasure."

Daniel's heart skipped a beat. What should he do? Babylonian food, meat—it wouldn't be cooked so a Jew could eat it. Food on the trip across the desert had been no problem—dried fruits and raisins, hard bread, cheeses, and water. But this food? Why, Babylonians would not know anything about the special rules God had made about the food Jews could eat—rules that would tell everybody Jews were different from other people. The animals had to be killed a certain way, and the blood drained out. Some animals Jews couldn't eat at all![12]But how would the Babylonians know? What should Daniel do? He had promised God he would do right no matter what happened. How could he eat this food and drink this wine when it was wrong?

"Hey, Daniel, aren't you hungry?" There was a smirk on the face of the Jewish lad who called across the room.

Daniel shook his head.

"Aw, come on, why aren't you eating?" The boy was determined to embarrass Daniel!

"I can't break God's laws and eat this food."

"Silly—who will ever know? Certainly not your father. Nor the priest."

"But God will know," Daniel said quietly.

Hananiah was just shovelling a big forkful of food in his mouth when he heard Daniel speak. "Psst! Azariah! Mishael! Wait! Daniel says this food isn't kosher!"

"Ugh!" Azariah said glumly. "My mouth was just watering for a big bite of that juicy beef!" But he put the fork down.

"What are you going to do, Daniel?"

"We'll see. Maybe Ashpenaz will give us some vegetables."

The other boys in the room began to jeer. "Hear, hear! Daniel thinks he's Jeremiah Junior! We left Jerusalem just so we could get away from that old prophet's poking his nose in our business, and got stuck with Daniel!"

Daniel flushed. "I'm not criticizing you for eating. I just am not going to eat this. I promised God I wouldn't defile myself. That's all there is to it."

"You and your God! Who cares about His laws? He doesn't care about us!"

"Yes, He does, and I am going to stay true to Him." Daniel put his plate down, and stepped over to where Ashpenaz stood. "Excuse me, sir. Could I talk to you?"

Ashpenaz nodded.

"Sir, you know we are Jews. And we are supposed to be different from other people." Daniel flushed under Ashpenaz' steady gaze. "God made certain laws about what we can eat. This food is forbidden to us—Sir, it tastes good, I don't mean that—but we aren't supposed to eat it." Out of the corner of his eye, Daniel saw Hananiah waving furiously at him and pointing at Azariah and Mishael. "—Oh, and my friends—they'd like permission not to eat it, too. Don't you have some plain old beans and peas, maybe some spinach, and plain old water we could have?"

Ashpenaz looked surprised, but he smiled kindly. "Belteshazzar, I like you. I like your spunk. But you are skin and bones. If I took you into the king looking like that, he'd chop off my head. No, Belteshazzar, you eat the king's food with thanks."

But Daniel didn't give up. When the next meal was served, he went to Melzar, the servant of Ashpenaz. "Sir, I got an idea."

Melzar grinned, and reached out and ruffled Daniel's hair. "That head of yours is full of ideas!"

"But this is a good one. Let's make a test, for ten days. Give us pulse to eat, just for ten days. Then see who's healthiest. It wouldn't hurt to try it just for ten days, would it?"

"All right. Ten days. You sure keep trying, don't you, Daniel?" Melzar cuffed him lightly on the shoulder.

For ten days Daniel and his friends ate the plain wholesome food they had requested. The rest of the boys ate the rich, seasoned meats and sweets and wines of the king. At the end of the ten days, it was easy to see who had won. Daniel and his friends were husky and clear-eyed. Their cheeks were rosy. The other boys were thin, listless, tired all the time. From that day on, Melzar gladly gave Daniel and his friends the food they requested.

God blessed the four boys in other ways, too. They learned the Chaldean language quickly. They understood their lessons. They remembered the dates and charts. They learned the movements of the stars and planets. When the royal summons came, long before the three years were up, Ashpenaz was not afraid to take them into the presence of the king.

The four young Jews bowed nervously. They tried to sneak a look at the king while their heads were bowed. They were dazzled by his glittering clothes, by his fierce eyes and intense, gravelly voice. The king asked them dozens of questions, hard questions, trick questions, rapid-fire. They answered him eagerly and courteously, in his own tongue.

The king waved a jewelled hand. "Enough! Enough! Ashpenaz, you chose well. These young men know ten times as much as any astrologer or magician anywhere in my kingdom. They shall serve me well." He turned to the boys. "From this day forward, Belteshazzar, Shadrach, Meshach and Abed-nego, you shall stand in my presence. You stand with the wise men of Babylon."

But that promotion, to be of the wise men of Babylon, intended to be an honor, nearly turned out to be a sentence of death to Daniel and his friends!

4. "Tell Me My Dream, or Else--!"

Heavy footsteps echoed on the cobblestone street. A drawn sword clanged against its scabbard. A lantern flickered in the darkness. A loud pounding on the door shook the house where Daniel lived with his three friends.

"Belteshazzar! Open the door in the name of the king!"

Daniel sat bolt upright in bed, his heart thumping. He snatched up a robe and hurried to the door. There stood Arioch, captain of the king's guard and—horrors!—the king's executioner!

"Belteshazzar," Arioch kept his voice sharp, trying not to show sympathy, "King Nebuchadnezzar has issued a decree that you and your companions are to be slain. I am here to obey his command."[13]

"Slain?. . .Killed?. . .But why?" Daniel's face paled even more. "Why should the king want to kill us?" Daniel was one of the chief wise men of Babylon, but he was still just a young man. He was far, far from his home, a captive in a strange land. He had tried to do right—had tried to serve the king faithfully. And now this! "Can you tell me why, Arioch?"

"The king has dreamed a dream this night. He cannot remember the dream, and it troubles him. He called for the magicians and astrologers and sorcerers, to tell him the dream. They can't tell him—say it's unfair. Just tell them the dream, they say, and they'll tell him what it means.

"But the king says if they were as wise as they claim, they ought to be able to tell him what he dreamed, says they are stalling for time." Arioch paused, then added glumly, "Of course, they can't tell the king his dream. Who could? A man would have to be God to know somebody else's dream! But the king is furious. He commands the death of every wise man in Babylon!" Arioch's eyes softened. "I'm sorry, young friend; I don't want to kill you. But it's my neck or yours."

Daniel put his hand on Arioch's arm. "Wait. . .Please wait. Take me to the king. I believe God will reveal the dream to me, if only the king will give me a little time."

"For your sake, Belteshazzar, I hope you are right. All right. Hurry along, here. Get dressed. We'll see if your glib tongue can buy your life."

Once in the king's presence, Daniel explained that

he did not know the dream, but he believed God would reveal it to him.

"Belteshazzar," the king answered gruffly, "if you will show me the dream, and what it means, I will give you many gifts and great honor. If you cannot tell me the dream, you will be cut in pieces!"

Daniel hurried back to his house. "Hananiah! Mishael! Azariah! Help me pray! Pray for mercy from the God of Heaven, so He will reveal the king's dream to me. Otherwise we die with the wise men of Babylon!"

How earnestly the four young men prayed! And that night, when Daniel went to sleep—imagine being able to sleep with the sentence of death hanging over you!—God answered their prayer. God sent a vision to Daniel. He saw all the king's dream. Then God told him what it all meant. Daniel jumped out of bed, and fell on his knees. "Thank you, oh, thank you, dear God, for answering our prayer. Thank you for giving me wisdom and might. Blessed be the name of God for ever and ever!"

Daniel hurried to the king's executioner. "Arioch! Good news! You must not kill the wise men! Take me to the king. I know the dream he dreamed!"

Together they hastened to the king's palace. They were brought into the king's presence immediately. They knelt, and then Arioch said, "O King Nebuchadnezzar, this young man, Belteshazzar, the captive of Judah, knows your dream. He will now tell you what it means."

Nebuchadnezzar turned his piercing eyes on Daniel. His face lighted up with hope. He was king of the greatest nation in the world, the first world empire, but he had been terribly frightened by this dream he could not remember! How could he please the gods if he did not know what they wanted? So he said to Daniel anxiously, "Are you able to tell me the dream I dreamed, and tell me as well what it means?"

Daniel smiled confidently. "I can, O King. It's no wonder your wise men and soothsayers couldn't tell you the dream. After all, they serve gods that are not gods—they are just sticks and stones, made with men's hands. But there is a God in Heaven who reveals secrets. He has given you this dream so you might know what will come to pass. O King, you dreamed you saw a great image, bright, shining, and terrible to see."

King Nebuchadnezzar gasped. "Yes, yes! Now I remember! That is what I dreamed! Go on!"

"The statue's head was gold. His arms and breast were silver." The king nodded—wordlessly. "His thighs were brass, his legs iron. His feet were mixed iron and clay. While you were looking at the image, a huge stone rolled down and hit it in the feet, shattering it to dust. The wind blew the dust away. Then the stone that broke the image became a great mountain, and filled up the whole earth."

King Nebuchadnezzar gripped the arms of his throne. "That's right! That is what I dreamed. But what does it mean? Oh, Belteshazzar, did your God tell you what it means?"

"Yes, O king, I can tell you what it means—oh, it's not because I am wise, but because God told me. King Nebuchadnezzar, God has a message for you. He has given you a great kingdom. He has made you ruler over all the children of men throughout the earth. The head of the gold statue represents you. Other kings will rule after you, but they will not be as great as you. The silver, brass and iron of the statue represent them. The last kingdom will break up into many small kingdoms. That's what the feet of the statue show—iron that won't mix with clay. All these little kingdoms will disappear, when the great Stone appears. The Stone represents God Himself, God who will make Himself Man. Then the God of Heaven will set up His own kingdom on earth, and it shall never be destroyed."

Nebuchadnezzar frowned. He kept clasping and unclasping his hands, and twisting the heavy rings on his fingers. "Is this really true, Belteshazzar? Will all this truly come to pass?"

"It will, O King. God Himself sent you this message. The dream is certain, and the interpretation is sure."

King Nebuchadnezzar threw himself off his throne, and knelt before Daniel. "Thank you, thank you, dear Belteshazzar. Your God is truly the God of all gods, and Lord of kings! Thank you for finding out my dream from Him!" The king clapped his hands. "Servants! Bring this man oblations and sweet odours! Bring the gifts I have prepared."

The servants streamed in, bearing velvets and jewels, and perfumes in caskets of alabaster.

"Belteshazzar," the king intoned solemnly, "for your wisdom I make you ruler over the whole province of Babylon, and chief of the governors over all the wise men of Babylon!"

Daniel looked at the man kneeling before him.

"But, sir, you know. . .surely you know I am a Jew."

Nebuchadnezzar waved his jewelled hand airily. "No matter."

"But my allegience must always be first of all to my God, my King, the God of my fathers. . . .You do understand, don't you, sir?"

Nebuchadnezzar gripped Daniel's arms so intensely it hurt. "I do understand, young Belteshazzar. It is that loyalty that makes you invaluable to me. You will not be lightly tempted to disloyalty."

Daniel dropped to his knees, and kissed the king's

hand. "I will be honored to serve you. . .and my God."

It was a promise Daniel never forgot. Many kings great and noble would he serve, but always, first of all, he would serve the great King of Heaven and earth, God Himself.

5. Tragic News of Home

King Nebuchadnezzar loved his great city of Babylon. He wanted it to be the most magnificent, the richest, and greatest in the world.

Babylon's history reached back nearly to the flood. For it was Nimrod, Noah's great grandson, that mighty hunter, who built it!¹⁴ The ruins of the ancient Tower of Babel could still be seen in Nebuchadnezzar's Babylon—a tumbled mass of bricks, abandoned when the men who began it could no longer understand the speech of one another.¹⁵

The city had risen many times to great power, and fallen, then, to many conquerors. Now King Nebuchadnezzar longed to make it more beautiful, more awe-inspiring, than any city in history. He hugged to himself the meaning of his vision—for Daniel had said the great image meant that Babylon really, truly was the center of the greatest empire in the world!

"Dear, faithful Daniel," Nebuchadnezzar said aloud, as he looked over his city. "Were it not for his faithfulness, I could not do all that is in my heart for this my city. Ashpenaz named him well indeed. He has protected his king!''

Daniel performed his task as chief ruler of the whole province with wisdom and simplicity. He seemed to know instinctively what to do, whatever the problem, whatever the need. He listened carefully to everyone who came. He asked questions that searched the heart. He made wise decisions. Yes, King Nebuchadnezzar was delighted with his choice as chief ruler of Babylon.

The wise men of Babylon were not so pleased. "Sir, I protest," one fat, balding wise man said to the king. "You have made this youth head over the wisest men of your kingdom!"

The king's lip curled. The deadly quietness of the king's voice should have warned the petulant man standing beside him.

"That young man revealed to me my dream and its meaning. You, sir, said it could not be done."

The wise man shrugged his shoulders and snapped his fingers carelessly. "Sheer chance, I say. He gave you vague, general words; they reminded you of your lost dream."

"Silence, you knave!" the king roared. "Say not one word more or my executioner Arioch shall visit you this day." The king drew a bony finger across his throat, and grimaced.

The wise man blanched. He could find no words to

answer the wrath of the king.

The king studied the man's face, now twisted with hate. "Why are you so set against young Belteshazzar? Do you forget he begged for your life when I would have killed you for not telling me my dream?"[16]

"Aye, I remember—and may be that is why I hate him," the old man muttered under his breath.

"Not a word more. I wish I had a hundred men as wise and good as Belteshazzar!"

The wise man turned, and shuffled away. But in his heart, he hoped he would some day get rid of Daniel and his friends.

With Daniel conducting the king's affairs so wisely, Nebuchadnezzar turned his attention to enlarging the borders of his kingdom. One by one, through the years, the nations of the world fell before his cruel, mighty army. Babylon became the great nation, full of power and glory, that Nebuchadnezzar's vision had foretold.

Eight years passed, from the day Daniel had been carried into Babylon a hostage. They had not been easy years for Daniel, but they had been worse for the people who stayed in Jerusalem. For Jehoiakim, king of Judah, who had faithfully promised to serve Nebuchadnezzar, and pay tribute to him, decided to rebel. He forgot the young men taken as hostage. He forgot the solemn vows he made to the king. When the

Prophet Jeremiah wrote down the very words of God, he dared to burn them in the fireplace, yet was he not afraid.[17] And he led the nation Judah deeper and deeper into sin.

Finally, King Nebuchadnezzar marched back to Jerusalem, captured Jehoiakim, and put him in chains to bring him back to Babylon. But before he could, Jehoiakim died. The angry people dragged his body out of Jerusalem, and threw it onto the garbage dump, as if it were an ass, just as the prophet Jeremiah had prophesied. No one wept when Jehoiakim died. He had been an evil, wicked man, and much sorrow had come upon his country because of his sin.[18]

King Nebuchadnezzar chose Jehoiakim's son, Jehoiachin, to be the new king. But, alas, he was as vile as his father. He was king for just three months, when King Nebuchadnezzar, in disgust, brought him to Babylon.[19]

It was a sad day for Daniel and his friends when King Jehoiachin limped down the Via Sacra of Babylon, the victory avenue, with his hands and his feet shackled in brass. Behind him marched his family, his officers, and his soldiers—nearly 10,000 people in all.

Daniel anxiously watched the sorrowful procession, looking for the familiar faces of the family he'd been separated from so long ago. He felt real pain of heart when he saw that the rest of the gold vessels and treasures had been taken from the House of God in Jerusalem. "I am the second most powerful man in this kingdom," he whispered to himself, "and I cannot spare my own king the humiliation of prison!" How much greater his sorrow would have been, had he known it would be 37 long, lonely years before Jehoiachin would be released from those iron bars!

That night Daniel talked with his friends, and pressed his head with his hands, as if to drive out the sight of that long line of Jews stumbling into captivity. "Is it right?" his voice broke with passion, "Is it right for me to serve King Nebuchadnezzar when my own people are his captives? But I must. It seems to be the will of God. But my beloved nation in captivity! Oh, dear God, help me to do right!"

Hananiah pulled Daniel's hands away from his face. "Daniel, oh, Daniel, please don't weep. You have always done only what you thought God told you to do."

Azariah put an arm around Daniel's shoulder. "And Daniel, don't you remember, the prophet Jeremiah told us Nebuchadnezzar was God's servant, to punish our people for their sins?"

"But how long?"

"Maybe the new king, Zedekiah will be a good king," Mishael said hopefully. It distressed him for Daniel, the one of the group who was usually so strong, to be so shaken by the sight he had seen.

"Zedekiah a good king? Jehoiakim's brother a good king? Sooner would the sun shine in the middle of the night!"

A knock on the door interrupted the conversation. Azariah answered it, and came back, waving a scroll. "News from home! Daniel, it's a letter from Jeremiah. Elasah, King Zedekiah's new ambassador to Nebuchadnezzar, brought it with him."

Daniel grabbed it eagerly, forgetting to be courteous. "Thus saith the Lord of hosts to the captives at Babylon," he read aloud, "Build ye houses and dwell in them, and plant gardens, and eat of them, and seek the peace of the city whither I have caused you to be carried away captives." Daniel stopped reading in emotion. Then "Pray unto the Lord for Babylon, for in the peace thereof shall ye have peace." [20]

"Whoopee," Azariah said joyfully. "Does he tell us how long?"

Daniel scanned the script quickly. "Yes, here it is. Seventy years. It can't happen yet, but it will."

Mishael sighed. "Isn't it wonderful that God sent this word right when we needed it?"

Daniel grinned. "It sure is. Oh, I am relieved! It is right for me to serve Nebuchadnezzar!"

It was good that Daniel had this assurance, for the next eleven years were the most terrible in the entire history of the nation of Judah. Zedekiah led the people into sins more vile and wicked than any his brother or his father had dreamed of. When the Prophet Jeremiah warned him, and begged him to repent, he listened instead to his princes, and they threw Jeremiah into a dark prison, into a deep hole filled with mud, so that he nearly died.[21]

Nor did the Jews who had already been captured repent because of their captivity. God sent the prophet Ezekiel to preach to them, but they made their hearts as hard as rocks against him.[22]

So it was that at last God gave the city of Jerusalem up. He sent King Nebuchadnezzar against the city of Jerusalem for the last time. King Nebuchadnezzar surrounded the city, and for 18 months would not let a soul inside or out. No one could get out to get food. People starved to death. Some gnawed their own flesh in hunger. Mothers ate their own babies. Brothers and sisters were afraid to go to sleep, for fear they would be killed and eaten by their own kin. Dreadful plagues stalked the streets, and men would stagger in the street, and die, and no one would have the strength to bury them. The horrible stench of death hovered over the city.

Late at night Zedekiah decided to make a break for it. He sneaked between the two walls near his garden, and ran toward Jericho. The Babylonian soldiers caught him, killed his soldiers, and dragged him before the king. Nebuchadnezzar had them kill his sons before his eyes, and then put out his eyes, and bind him in chains for the long trip across the desert to Babylon. And there Zedekiah died. Never again, never again, would a king sit on the throne of Judah until the day—how many, many years hence?—when the Lord Jesus Christ Himself would rule the whole world from that throne!

6. In the Shadow of the Burning Fiery Furnace

Outside Babylon, on the wide, level plain of Dura, Nebuchadnezzar built a huge gold statue.[24] It soared over ninety feet into the air, and seemed almost to touch the sky. You could see it from miles away, as the sunlight flashed on the solid gold.

King Nebuchadnezzar rubbed his hands with delight. He sent word to the governors, the princes, the judges, the treasurers to come from all the provinces. "Now for a dedication that will surpass every celebration anybody has ever dreamed of!" There would be a great orchestra to play. Every man would wear the finest silks and velvets he could muster. Every man would bow at the sound of the orchestral fanfare, and any who dared not to bow down would be cast into a terrible furnace of fire. Ah, what a celebration that would be! His pages hastened throughout the city streets with the proclamation.

Hananiah, Azariah, and Mishael heard the words,

and looked at one another in consternation. "That image! He intends for us to bow down to it! That we cannot do!"

The other two shook their heads. "Never."

"But," Hananiah moved his shoulders uneasily, as if he could already feel the heat of the furnace nearby, "but you know how angry the king gets—if he sets his mind to it, no one can change it."

Azariah bit his lip. "Sometimes he acts like a mad man when he is angry."

"I wish Daniel were here—he'd tell us what to do."

Mishael held up his hand impatiently. "We already know what to do."

"Yes, but I keep remembering how horrible the heat was the last time."

"You mean when Nebuchadnezzar burned up Zedekiah and Ahab?" [25]

Azariah whistled. "Nobody could save them from that fire."

"But don't forget—they were false prophets."

"True. Still—" It was as if that burning fiery furnace stood right beside them, the flames licking out, reaching for them greedily!

Mishael shuddered. Then he squared his shoulders, and took a deep breath. "I'll tell you what I'm going to do. I am going to stay true to God even if it means burning in that furnace. I will not bow down to Nebuchadnezzar's image."

Azariah reached to clasp his hand. "Me, too!"

"And me," said Hananiah.

It was with hearts beating hard that the three men walked out to the plain of Dura to stand before the golden image, summoned by the king.

King Nebuchadnezzar sat in his gaily-decorated tent, and looked out across the field. Everything was exactly as he planned it! The huge golden image was dazzling in the sunlight, blinding those who looked too long at it. The great orchestra was assembled. And, stretched out across the plain, leaders of all the provinces ruled by King Nebuchadnezzar waited in humble submission. On this great day they would bow before Nebuchadnezzar's huge idol.

Everything awaited the king's command. Cornetists stood with their cornets at their mouths. The multitude was in regular rows. And the huge furnace, its fire already ablaze, waited nearby. Today the unity of the world empire in one religion would be manifested!

King Nebuchadnezzar motioned for the ceremony to begin. The orchestra blared. As the sound reached the waiting people, they fell to their faces on the ground. Their kneeling bodies looked like a giant ocean wave sweeping across the plain.

The king stood proudly, tasting his victory. Oh, it was sweet to be King of Babylon! Then he became aware of a commotion behind him. "O king," a

Chaldean said hatefully, "did you not say that every man must worship the golden image?"

"I did," said the king. "Who dared not obey?"

"Those three Jews, O King, whose Babylonian names are Shadrach, Meshach, and Abed-nego. They have refused to bow down to your golden image."

The king's face turned red. "How dare they? Bring them here!"

Within a few minutes Hananiah, Mishael, and Azariah were thrust at the king's feet. His voice shook with anger. "Is it true, O Shadrach, Meshach, and Abed-nego, that you will not serve my gods?"

The three Hebrews did not flinch. "Yes, sir."

The king waited for their blubbering apologies, but, instead, they stood quietly before him.

The king's eyes burned with anger. "Because you have served me well, in my mercy I will give you one more chance. The orchestra will play again. If you worship the image, well. If not, I will throw you into yonder furnace. Do you understand? What god, even your God, can deliver you from that fire?"

Hananiah's eyes were drawn irresistibly to the fiery furnace. Its hot heart burned red with glowing coals, and cinders spewed into the air. It hadn't been easy, this morning, to say he would not bow down to Nebuchadnezzar's image. It was a hundred times harder now, standing by that blasting heat, to say he would not bow. He shut his eyes a second , and begged

God to help him be brave. Then he looked at Azariah and Mishael. They were afraid as he—he could tell by their flushed faces, and their tense mouths—but they were both shaking their heads. No! They would not bow to the idol!

Hananiah turned to the king, and looked him steadily in the face. "O Nebuchadnezzar, we do not need any time to think about it. We do not need a second chance. We will not bow down to your image. If you throw us into the furnace, our God whom we serve is able to deliver us from it—and He will deliver us. But if He does *not* deliver us, if we die in that furnace, we want you to know, O King, we still are not going to serve your gods!"

King Nebuchadnezzar turned with rage. His voice was harsh. "Guards! GUARDS! Heat the furnace seven times hotter. HURRY! In fear of your lives, Hurry!"

The frightened men heaped fuel and oil on the flames. It rose into a monstrous, blistering pillar of fire.

"Tie them up! Throw them in! HURRY! We'll see them suffer for their God!" the king thundered. Frightened, the soldiers fumbled and twisted the ropes, forgetting to take off the men's hats and coats. As they thrust them into the furnace, the flames flared up, suffocating the soldiers. Hananiah, Azariah, and

Mishael fell into a heap in the center of the white-hot coals of fire.

King Nebuchadnezzar expected to see the men writhe in pain, and die. He peered through the licking flames. What he saw made him gasp. "Did we not throw *three* men into the furnace?"

His counsellors nodded.

Nebuchadnezzar squinted through the flames. He counted with a trembling finger. "Lo," he whispered with awe, "I see four men loose, walking in the midst of the fire, and they have no hurt." His voice dropped lower yet. "And the form of the fourth man is like the Son of God!"

Could it be that the God of Heaven and earth, the God of gods, had made Himself Man, as the wise man Daniel had prophesied? These men who scorned the worst that Nebuchadnezzar could threaten—did God Himself walk with them? "The form of the fourth man is like the Son of God!"

Nebuchadnezzar buried his face in his hands. There was a long, long silence while he sat thus. Finally he stepped to the mouth of the furnace. His voice was not commanding now, not harsh and kingly. Rather, he said quietly, pleading, "Shadrach, Meshach, and Abed-nego, ye servants of the most high God, come forth!"

The three young men stepped briskly out of the furnace. People crowded around them, astonished beyond speaking. Though the fire had burned their ropes, it had not touched them. Their clothes were not burned, not even charred. Their hair was not singed. There was no odor of smoke on them at all!

King Nebuchadnezzar was overwhelmed. He groped for words. "Blessed be the God of Shadrach, Meshach, and Abed-nego! He sent his angel, and delivered his servants that trusted in him. They yielded their bodies to be burned, rather than obey my command. They would not serve any god except their own God!"

He turned to the scribe beside him. "Write this down. I make a decree. Any people, nation, or language which says anything amiss against the God of Shadrach, Meshach, and Abed-nego will be killed and his house knocked down. There is no other god, in any nation, that can save like this!" Then the king gave the three Hebrew men important new jobs in governing the province of Babylon.

The three friends could hardly wait for Daniel to get back to Babylon so they could tell him about it. They told him about their new jobs. They told him about the wonderful testimony King Nebuchadnezzar had given to the God of Heaven and earth. But the thing they couldn't tire of telling, the thing they remembered with greatest joy was that, when they were thrown down into the terrible fire, they discovered that God Himself had come down to walk with them through it!

"Who's afraid of the king's hottest fire," Hananiah asked joyfully, "if God Himself walks through it with you?"

7. Eagles' Feathers and Animal Claws

King Nebuchadnezzar was afraid—terribly afraid, and that hadn't happened to him in years. Tonight the great king of Babylon struggled awake, terrified by a dream. He threw back the covers.

"A light!" he called hoarsely to his body servant. "Bring a light!"

He ran his hands through his graying hair, hands trembling. Why should he, Nebuchadnezzar, be afraid? There was not a nation on earth strong enough to meet him in battle. He had conquered them all, all of them, and their kings lay that night in Babylonian dungeons, fettered in brass. The great city of Babylon was surrounded by walls within walls, reaching nearly to the sky, guarded by the finest soldiers in the kingdom. No, there was not a mortal on earth he need fear.

Nor did Nebuchadnezzar need to fear the gods, either. Babylon glittered with the temples he had built to all the gods of the nations he had conquered. When he brought a king into captivity, he carried their gods into captivity as well.[26]They were all safely inside the walls of Babylon. No man could use their power to hurt him. To his own god, Merodach, Nebuchadnezzar had built a temple as beautiful as man's imagination could devise, made with pure gold, inlaid with precious jewels. Only to the God of Israel had he not built a temple, because Daniel, his chief wise man, said his God would not dwell in a temple made with man's hands.

Nevertheless, tonight Nebuchadnezzar was afraid. He wiped the cold sweat off his forehead. "Call my wise men. I've dreamed a dream. I must know what it means."

Nebuchadnezzar's wise men glided into the king's presence clasping their hands, and bowing, and looking very, very wise. They looked at the king, with troubled face as he told them his dream. "Tell me," the king begged, "what does the dream mean?"[27]

The wise men stared at each other, careful not to let their eyes betray their thoughts. What *did* the dream mean? They drew into a little circle in the corner, out of earshot of the king.

"What shall we tell him the dream means?"

"Oh, just make up something—any old thing, like we usually do."

"Wait!" a feeble old man cautioned. "I fear this is

no ordinary dream! What if it is the gods who speak to him?"

Others nodded. "I thought the same as I heard the king speak. I believe the gods are trying to tell him something."

"Strange you should say that. I felt it, too. Remember, years ago, when the king stood at the parting of the roads to Rabbath Ammon and Jerusalem? We had decided among us we would say he was to attack Rabbath Ammon—do you remember?"

"Yes, I remember. He made his arrows bright, and consulted the images, and looked in the liver. When I opened my mouth to tell him what we had agreed upon, the words changed themselves as they came out of my mouth, to say he should attack Jerusalem." [28]

They all agreed. "We dare not pretend to know what this dream means!"

They turned back to the king, and shook their heads, surprised and baffled. "Sir, we cannot tell what the dream means."

Nebuchadnezzar was disturbed. He had to know the dream's meaning. What could he do? Who would know? Who? Daniel! Daniel would know! Why didn't he think of him sooner? Why? Nebuchadnezzar had not called for Daniel often in recent years. Daniel was too honest, too straight-forward. It was easier to listen to the flattery of his wise men. But now! Who wanted flattery? "Call Belteshazzar!" the king demanded. "Tell him to hurry!"

Shortly Daniel bowed respectfully before the king.

"Belteshazzar, I know the spirit of the holy gods lives in you. No secret troubles you. Tonight I have dreamed a dream. I saw a huge tree—it seemed to touch the sky. Beautiful fruit grew on every branch. Birds lived in it; animals lived under it. They ate of its fruit. But a watcher, a holy one, came down from Heaven. He cried out, 'Chop the tree down! Lop off the branches! Scatter the fruit, and drive away the birds and beasts. But leave the stump. Let a beast's heart be given to it, and let seven times pass over it. This is decreed by the holy ones so everyone will know that the Most High God Himself decides who will be king.' "

Nebuchadnezzar searched Daniel's face. "Please, dear friend, tell me what it means."

Daniel stood silently. As he saw God's meaning in the dream, tears sprang to his eyes. He struggled to speak, but the words would not come out. For an hour, he stood without being able to talk.

Nebuchadnezzar spoke gently. "Please don't be troubled. Just tell me what the dream means."

"Your enemies will be pleased to hear of this dream, King Nebuchadnezzar. The tree represents you. Nations have rested in your shadow, and you have fed them. But now, you are to be given a heart like a beast, and driven into the field like an ox, until you learn that God is the One who made you great." Daniel held his hands out to the king. "O King, let my counsel be acceptable to you. Break off your sins, and turn to God. Perhaps He will postpone this judgment."

The king listened, deeply disturbed, but then he dismissed Daniel. He liked Daniel. He trusted what he said. But pride in his kingdom, his accomplishment was a great temptation.

Nebuchadnezzar tried to forget the dream. He filled his days with designing and planning, building and planting in his beloved Babylon.

A year went by. Nebuchadnezzar walked in his palace, and looked out over the city he had made beautiful. "Is not this great Babylon, that I have built for the house of the kingdom by the might of my power, and for the honour of my majesty?"

And as the words fell from his proud lips, a voice from Heaven answered, "Nebuchadnezzar! The kingdom has been taken away from you!" Suddenly, Nebuchadnezzar was not the brilliant general, not the great king. He began to act like an animal, crawling on his hands and knees, making growling sounds. Frightened and disgusted, his counsellors drove him out of the palace into the fields.

His hair grew long and tangled. His fingernails began to curve like animal claws. Rain soaked his body, and the blistering sun burned it. His eyes stared dully through matted hair. Day and night he wandered through the fields, nibbling grass, sleeping under the stars, drinking from the river. For seven long years, Nebuchadnezzar, the great king of Babylon, lived like a useless, mindless beast.

But at the end of seven years, Nebuchadnezzar lifted his vacant, staring eyes up to God. Somehow his darkened animal heart cried out to God, and God had mercy on him. His understanding returned to him. He knew who he was, and he knew who God was, that He was the One Great God of Heaven and Earth, and he loved Him and worshipped Him.

How gladly Nebuchadnezzar's counsellors heard the news! (For the kingdom had suffered greatly in the seven years of his absence.) They led him back to the palace with shouts of joy, and robed him in satins and brocades, and trimmed his nails, and cut his hair. When they were done, Nebuchadnezzar, the greatest king of the greatest nation in the world, ascended again his golden throne. He lifted a hand, to stop their celebration. With a quiet voice, he said, "I Nebuchadnezzar praise and extol and honour the King of Heaven, all whose works are truth, and his ways judgment: and those that walk in pride he is able to abase."

Beside the throne, on the king's right hand again, stood Daniel. The king turned to him, and hugged him tightly. And Daniel silently counted back through the years he had prayed for this day. As a young man, forty years ago, Daniel had asked God to touch Nebuchadnezzar's heart. Today at long, long last, that prayer had been answered. Nebuchadnezzar, King of Babylon, had turned with all his heart to God, the only true God!

8. Daniel Dreams of Strange, Wild Beasts

Would Israel be restored at last? Would their captivity end? How many years ago it had been that Daniel, a youth, through eyes dimmed with tears, and throat choked with sobs, watched his beloved Jerusalem drop from sight behind the hills that surround it. Now would he let the Jewish people who wished to go, return to their ancient home in Jerusalem?

Not yet, for God had told Jeremiah to prophesy that they must stay in Babylon for seventy years. No, the sin of Judah had been great. Their punishment must be great.

King Nebuchadnezzar died. He was buried with somber ceremony, in great grief. It was hard for any man to take the place of Nebuchadnezzar. He had been a brilliant, strong ruler. Several men seized the throne, but none could hold it long.

Evil-merodach was made king for a season. Early

in his reign he called to a guard, "Bring forth Jehoiachin, king of Judah, from his prison cell." Jehoiachin stumbled into the presence of the king, blinking in the bright sunlight. For thirty-seven years Jehoiachin had stared through the iron bars of the dungeon, chained, hungry, tormented by memories. Now he was a gray-headed man, 55 years old, his face lined with sadness.

King Evil-Merodach looked down at him kindly. "Jehoiachin, this day do I lift up your head out of the prison. You shall sit on a throne, above the thrones of the other kings captive in Babylon. You will eat at my table. I will supply all your needs for you and your family for the rest of your life."

King Jehoiachin listened to the words in disbelief. But servants brought a new robe, and took away his smelly prison rags. He was brought to a pleasant apartment in the palace, and there he lived in comfort until his death.

After Evil-Merodach died, again there was civil war over the throne of Babylon. Finally Belshazzar, a kinsman of Nebuchadnezzar, became king. But he was a wicked, evil man. He filled the palace with his wicked friends. They got drunk together, and worshipped the heathen idols which filled Babylon. Daniel served him faithfully, but Belshazzar never called him into his presence, to ask his advice or help.

Belshazzar's wickedness deeply troubled Daniel.

How long would all this last? Would there ever come a king to power who would love God? Would evil men always control the earth?

In the first year of Belshazzar's reign, Daniel went to bed one night, trying to figure out all these things. [30] He fell into a troubled sleep, and dreamed of strange, queer beasts. First he saw a lion with eagles' wings, standing on its hind feet. It had a man's heart. Next Daniel saw a ferocious bear, chewing on three ribs torn from an animal's body. Then came a swift leopard, with four heads, and wings like a bird. Then another animal sprang up—not like any animal ever seen on earth! It chewed up all the other beasts with its huge teeth of iron, and crushed their mangled bodies under its sharp claws. As Daniel watched, something fearfully strange happened. From among its ten horns, another horn pushed up. It had eyes like a man, and mouth that spewed out horrible curse words.

Then, to Daniel's infinite relief, all the thrones of the beasts were knocked down. A great, flaming throne was set up, and the Ancient of Days, God Himself, sat down on it. Millions of angels crowded around Him. They brought him the books where all the sins had been written down, and they were read aloud. Then the terrible beast with the ten horns was killed, and the Son of Man came. To Him were given all the kingdoms of the world.

"What does it all mean?" Daniel's heart cried. "I don't understand what it means!"

An angel came to him, and spoke quietly. "Daniel, the animals represent different kingdoms. The lion represents the kingdom of Babylon. It will be destroyed by another kingdom, and that one will be destroyed by another. At the end, the most terrible kingdom of all will be destroyed. Then Jesus, the Son of the Ancient of Days, will be made King for ever and ever."

When Daniel woke up, he thought and thought about the dream. What did it mean? He couldn't talk to anyone about it. When would all this come about? Daniel prayed, and worked, and pondered over the dream for two whole years. Then God sent another dream.

"This will not all happen right away, Daniel," the angel Gabriel explained. "This will happen in the end time. All you need to know right now is that the kingdom of Babylon will be conquered by the two kings of Media and Persia."

And though Daniel did not know it, already, miles across the burning desert to the east, mysterious things were happening that would make that prophecy come true.

9. Who Is That Child?

In the kingdom of the Medes, far to the east of Babylon, King Astyages sat on his royal throne, and listened to the tale of one of his noblemen. The man was sputtering with rage.

"See, sire, the marks of the whip the cowherd's son used on my son's back." His finger traced the red welts.

The king frowned. "The son of a cowherd did this? Why?"

The boy burst in, blustering and pouting. "It began as a game. We elected him to be king. But he gave me a job I didn't want to do and when I refused, he whipped me."

"Why did you not deal with the cowherd as befits your station as a nobleman?" the king asked the father. "You have the right to punish by death any you deem deserve it."

"Sire, this cowherd belongs to you. I did not think it wise to touch the property of the king, howsoever much he deserved death."

The king's face darkened in anger. "One of my

vassals did this to a nobleman's son? Bring this
cowherd and his son in to me."

The cowherd entered, trembling, grasping the arm
of the ten-year-old boy beside him. The boy patted his
father's arm reassuringly, and then looked up into the
king's face solemnly. He did not seem to be afraid in
the least.

The king stared at the boy in shock. His eyes traced
the firm profile, the erect, composed bearing. The boy
was a very copy of himself! The aura of a king
surrounded him. Had not even his playmates sensed
this, and made obeisance to him? This child was a
king! The king jabbed a finger at the boy.

"Who is this child? Who *is* he?"

"Sire," the cowherd whispered, "he is my son."

"You lie," the king said with vehemence. "Who is
this child?"

The cowherd wilted before the king's glare. His
voice dropped lower. "Sire, he is . . .he is my son."

"Guards!" the king roared. "Take this man to the
rack. Tear the truth from his lying lips! I must know
whence this child comes."

The cowherd crumpled in a heap before the king.
"Nay, sir," he said brokenly, "not the rack. I. . .I
lied. . .for the sake of this bonnie lad, I lied."

"Then he is not your son?"

"Nay. Ten years ago this child was brought to me
by Harpagus, your prime minister. He told me to

expose the child to the wild beasts out on the mountains, so they would kill it. It had been commanded him to do it, he said, but the child was so fair he could not bring himself to do it."

The king shot a glance at his prime minister. Animosity hung like the blade of a sword between them.

The cowherd saw the look. "Nay, sire, please do not hold him to account. It was my own fault. That very day my wife had given birth to a dead baby. To ease her pain, and comfort her, I gave her this child to nurse. I exposed the body of my dead baby son to the wild beasts, and afterwards gave its bloody bones to Harpagus. He never guessed it was not the child he had given me."

The king's voice lashed out like a whip. "Did you not know the child's origin?"

"Nay, sire. I knew he was of noble blood because of his rich clothing." His glance swept lovingly over the figure of the child beside him. "I have known it more clearly, since, for he carries himself as a king."

The king lurched back to his throne, stricken. "Aye, he is a king. This child is my flesh. He is the son of my daughter. Before his birth, I dreamed he would seize my throne. It was my intent to murder him so that could not happen. But the gods have intervened. Cyrus still lives. So be it." The king covered his eyes with his hands, and sighed heavily.

"See that he is taken to his mother. His life is secure. He shall live."

King Astyages did not try again to take the life of Cyrus. But he was furious with Harpagus, the officer he had commanded to kill the child. In his fury, to pay Harpagus back for the disaster he was sure to come, Astyages killed the son of Harpagus. He had his body cooked, and served to Harpagus for supper, and did not tell him until afterward he had eaten the flesh of his own child. Such was the wickedness of King Astyages, king of the Medes. Harpagus pretended not to care. He pretended he thought the king had acted in wisdom. But he made a promise to himself. "Someday, King Astyages, I will pay you back, and it shall be through the child whose life I saved."

Cyrus was taken to Persia, where his father and mother lived. He did not see his grandfather, the king, through those many years. But when he grew to manhood, Harpagus sent him a message. It was a secret message, hidden in the entrails of an hare he had killed, so no enemy would see it, and tell the king. "Now, O Cyrus, is the time to repay King Astyages for trying to kill you. I have raised up an army, and will help you fight."

Cyrus read the letter thoughtfully. Already he had the loyalty of the men in the Persian army. Why not accept the offer of Harpagus? He did. The two men united their forces. They defeated the army of the

Medes. King Astyages was captured. As he sat amid his chains, he remembered the dream he'd dreamed so long ago. It had come true. The child had grown up to seize the throne! Surely now he faced torture and death at the hands of the man he had so cruelly wronged. But he was mistaken. Cyrus repaid him with kindness. He spared the king's life, and let his grandfather live in his court in peace.

Cyrus became a mighty king. Under the leadership of Harpagus, the Mede, the Persian armies stormed across the lands, defeating all their enemies. Now these two men, one a Mede, and the other a Persian, turned their faces toward Babylon, that nation that was still the mightiest nation on earth.[31]

Now Belshazzar, grandson of King Nebuchadnezzar, knew the armies of the Medes and Persians marched toward Babylon. But he was not afraid. Were not the walls of Babylon so thick two chariots could run abreast on them around the city? Were not those walls so high no ladder could be built that would scale them? Were not the city's graneries filled with grain? Did not the Euphrates River run through the heart of the city, so they had no fear of thirst? Let the Medes and the Persians come! Babylon could withstand years of siege! Lock the city gates! Bring forth the wine! Let us eat and drink and be merry, for nothing else matters, and soon enough we will be old and in our graves!

But there was something terribly important Belshazzar did not know. Oh, he could have known it. He *should* have known it, but he was too careless in having fun to bother with such minor things. Belshazzar did not know that God had told Daniel plainly that the kings of Media and Persia would capture Babylon. Daniel had dreamed about a ram that had two horns that "pushed westward, and northward, and southward; so that no beasts might stand before him, neither was there any that could deliver out of his hand; but he did according to his will, and became great." Then the angel Gabriel said plainly to Daniel, "The ram which thou sawest having two horns are the kings of Media and Persia." [32] Babylon was doomed!

Belshazzar could have known all this. Indeed, two hundred years before, the prophet Isaiah had written down the name of the man who would bring the children of Israel back from their captivity, before they had even gone in to captivity! "Thus saith the Lord," Isaiah had written "That saith of Cyrus, He is my shepherd, and shall perform all my pleasure: even saying to Jerusalem, Thou shalt be built; and to the temple, Thy foundation shall be laid. Thus saith the Lord to his anointed, Cyrus. . .I have even called thee by thy name: I have surnamed thee, though thou hast not known me." [33]

Isaiah, writing down the very words God told him to write, said, "Behold, I will stir up the Medes against them, which shall not regard silver; and as for gold, they shall not delight in it. Their bows also shall dash the young men to pieces; and they shall have no pity on the fruit of the womb; their eye shall not spare children. And Babylon, the glory of the kingdoms, the beauty of the Chaldees' excellency, shall be as when God overthrew Sodom and Gomorrah." [34]

Belshazzar should have known this. He should have repented, but he would not. So it was that God set about to pay back Babylon for the terrible way it had treated His people, the Jews.

While Belshazzar partied in the palace, far upstream on the Euphrates River, the attacking army moved quietly to its deadly work.

10. A Mysterious Hand Writes on the Wall

The armies of the Medes and Persians crouched at the gates of Babylon, waiting to pounce, but King Belshazzar was still not afraid. In fact, to show how unafraid he was, he would give the biggest party ever! He invited a thousand of his lords. They would feast together, and worship their idols of wood and stone, and thumb their noses at the Medes and Persians outside the gates!

Meanwhile Darius, the Mede (who may have been the same man as Harpagus) and Cyrus, the Persian, eyed the massive Babylonian walls.

"Darius, what say you? How shall we enter the city?"

Darius shook his head. "Can't use ladders. The walls are too high. To build mounts would take years—there is not enough wood here."

"Notice the River Euphrates flows under those walls. Could our soldiers swim under them?"

Darius shook his head. "I think not."

Cyrus agreed. "When I walked into the city last month, disguised as a beggar, I noted that those walls must be fifty feet thick. Few of our men could swim that far under water."

"If we could only dry up the River!" Darius laughed.

"Wait a minute! Perhaps we can," Cyrus said seriously.

"Dry up the Euphrates? But how?"

"Remember the story of Nitocris, queen of Babylon? She wanted to build a bridge across the river in the midst of Babylon."

Darius's eyes lighted up. "Oh, yes. She made an artificial lake, didn't she, upstream, where the marshes are?"

"And blocked the river, and sent the water into the lake she had dug."

"So the Euphrates ceased to flow through Babylon. . .Right! We can do the same. We will march *under* the walls of invincible Babylon."

Cyrus put a hand on the shoulder of Darius. "Let us to the work!" [35]

The armies set to work. They used their horses to drag to the river huge blocks of stone. They scraped back the earth that banked the river against the marshes. The water began to trickle into the old, dried-up lake. Slowly, so slowly that no one in

Babylon seemed to notice, the level of water flowing through Babylon dropped. If only they had noticed, the guards in Babylon could have locked the gates along the river, inside the city walls. Then the Medes and Persians still could not have gotten into the city. But the guards, like Belshazzar, thought they were perfectly safe inside Babylon's mighty walls. They never troubled themselves to keep awake, or to man the gates.

Belshazzar's party was a huge success. Never had the palace halls echoed with such laughter, such singing! Never had the wine flowed more freely. Never had the king been so drunk. He beckoned dizzily to a servant.

"I'm tired of this wine. I think I know what will improve the flavor. Bring to me the vessels of gold and silver which my father Nebuchadnezzar brought from the temple in Jerusalem." [36]

The vessels were brought—those holy, beautiful vessels, designed by the hand of God Himself to be used in the worship of Him alone!—and the Babylonians filled those lovely vessels to the brim with stupefying wine! Belshazzar waved his cup. The liquid slopped over the side, and splashed on those around him.

"Ah, you beautiful thing!" he said lazily to the cup. "You are worthy of my gods!"

But as he tried to focus his bloodshot eyes on the

cup, his glance fell on the wall across the room. A hand—just a hand, nothing more—was writing in large characters on the plaster of the wall beside the lighted candlestick. The king gaped in stunned surprise, and squinted as he tried to read the writing. What did it say? He could not tell. What ghost had written those horrible, meaningless words? His arms and legs turned to rubber. He fell back in his seat. His teeth chattered so it was hard to make the words come out. "Call my astrologers!" he cried. "Hurry! Tell them whoever can read this writing, I will give him a chain of gold, and clothing of scarlet, and make him third ruler in the kingdom."

The wise men hurried to the king's side. They gawked at the writing. But none could read a word. Then Belshazzar truly was terrified.

Belshazzar's queen mother heard the awful news. She hurried to the banquet hall. "O king," she said, breathing heavily, "there is a man in your kingdom in whom is the spirit of the holy gods. Your father Nebuchadnezzar made him chief wise man. Call Daniel, named Belteshazzar. He will be able to tell you what the writing means."

It had been years since Daniel had been summoned into the king's presence, for Belshazzar did not want to listen to the words of a man who said, "Thus saith the Lord." Nevertheless, Daniel came quickly to the king's side. He slowly read the writing on the wall, and then looked into the face of the king.

"Come, come, can you read the writing? I'll give you many gifts if you can."

"Yes, O king, I can tell you what the writing means. But keep your gifts. I don't want them. You know, O king, that the Most High God gave your father Nebuchadnezzar a great kingdom. He was the greatest man in the kingdom, and that kingdom the greatest in the world. He could do anything his heart desired. But when he lifted up his heart, then God cast him off his throne. He wandered around like a beast in the fields, until he learned that the Most High God rules in the kingdom of men. God decides who will rule.

"Now, King Belshazzar, you knew all this. But you have deliberately lifted up your heart against God. You praised gods made with men's hands, gods that can't see or hear. You would not glorify the true God of Heaven and earth, the God who holds your breath in His hands!"

Belshazzar interrupted impatiently. "What does that writing mean?"

Daniel read it aloud: "MENE, MENE, TEKEL, UPHARSIN. MENE means God has ended your reign, and your kingdom. TEKEL means God has judged you, and you have been found wanting.

PERES means your kingdom is given to the Medes and Persians.''

It was hard to tell, looking on, if the message frightened Belshazzar yet more, or if the wine had so drugged his senses he was unable to be afraid. He did command that the robe be brought, and a proclamation made that Daniel should be third ruler in the kingdom. But even as the proclamation was made, even as the scarlet robe was draped on Daniel's shoulders, and the chain of authority hung about his neck, the armies of the Medes and Persians were wading through the knee-deep waters of the Euphrates, underneath the impregnable walls of Babylon! Silently, like ghosts, they overpowered the unsuspecting guards, and swarmed into the city.

In that night, Belshazzar, the king who lifted up his heart against God, was slain. Darius, the Mede, took the kingdom. That very night came true the prophecy of the hand that had written on the wall.

11. Unconquerable Babylon Conquered

On the marble floor of the great banquet hall Belshazzar, King of Babylon, lay in a pool of blood, slain by a Mede's silver-shafted sword. Above his body, etched in the plaster of the wall were words written by the finger of God: "Weighed in the balance—and found wanting!"

The soldiers of Darius the Mede swept through the littered hall, saving those who surrendered, killing those who resisted. They stopped suddenly before a tall, noble figure who stood quietly surveying the scene. He was dressed in scarlet. A costly chain of gold was draped around his neck. (He had told Belshazzar to keep his gifts—what good was a gold chain of authority when the king who gave it to him would be dead ere the night ended?)

Daniel was old now, over eighty years old. His shoulders were stooped with the burdens of the years. The old empire had fallen. A new empire had begun.

It had happened exactly as the visions had foretold!

What would happen to Daniel now? He did not know. But he did know that the God of Heaven was still in control, and that whatever happened would be His will. So Daniel faced the soldiers with a steady, calm gaze. Ashpenaz, eunuch of the king, had seen that quiet confidence in the young Daniel. King Nebuchadnezzar had seen it in the mature man Daniel, and so had unhesitatingly entrusted to him the highest affairs of the kingdom. Now, when the soldiers brought Daniel the aged to their king Darius, Darius looked into his gentle face, and was attracted to him at once.

Darius would need wise counsel as he brought together the sprawling kingdoms he had conquered, and Daniel would be the one who would supervise it. Darius chose 120 princes to rule over the various provinces, and set over them three presidents. Then he chose as chief president the Hebrew captive, Daniel. [37]

Daniel worked faithfully for King Darius, just as he had the other kings for the 68 years he had lived in Babylon. Because he loved God, and because he trusted God's wisdom, he tried not to complain. But oh, how he longed for his old home, Jerusalem! And how he wept as he read God's Word, as he realized the sins of his people were still what kept them from their homeland.

One day Daniel was reading the book of God which

the prophet Jeremiah had written down. What he read made his heart pound furiously. "For thus saith the Lord," the Book said, "that after seventy years be accomplished at Babylon I will visit you, and perform my good word toward you, in causing you to return to this place."[38] Seventy years? Daniel calculated swiftly. He had been held captive in Babylon for exactly sixty-eight years. The captivity of his people was nearly over!

Daniel dropped to his knees. He began to weep and pray, confessing his sins, and the sins of his people. How long he prayed, he didn't know. He didn't eat; he didn't work; he just prayed. Then in the evening, just as the sun was setting, he felt a touch on his shoulder. He looked up. It was the angel Gabriel!

"Daniel," the angel said tenderly, "God has heard your prayers. He has sent me to tell you what is going to happen, for He loves you very dearly.

"Know therefore and understand, that from the going forth of the commandment to restore and build Jerusalem unto the Messiah the Prince shall be seven weeks, and threescore and two weeks: the street shall be built again, and the wall, even in troublous times. And after threescore and two weeks shall Messiah be cut off, but not for himself; and the people of the prince that shall come shall destroy the city and the sanctuary, and the end thereof shall be with a flood, and unto the end of the war desolations are determined." [39]

Daniel was greatly troubled by the vision. What did Gabriel mean? He understood the part about the command to rebuild Jerusalem. Jerusalem had been destroyed by Nebuchadnezzar. A new king—would it be Darius?—would command that the city be rebuilt. A certain number of years would pass, and then the Messiah would come. How long would it be before the Messiah could come? Daniel thought again about the prophecy: "seven weeks of years and sixty-two weeks of years." That would make sixty-nine weeks of years. If a week of days was seven days, he figured, then a week of years would be seven years. Daniel feverishly multiplied it out: 69 x 7 = 483. Four hundred and eighty-three years after a king, whoever it would be, issued the decree to rebuild Jerusalem, then the Messiah, the Prince, would give His life.

Oh, how Daniel longed to see that Messiah—the One anointed by God to redeem the world from sin. For he had read in the Scriptures all the promises God had made about Him. In the book of Genesis, God promised the Redeemer would come through the seed of the woman.[40] In Deuteronomy, He had promised a Prophet, from among the brethren, but like Moses.[41] Daniel didn't understand how it would all work out, but he knew he had to know the Messiah so his sins could be forgiven.

Daniel was very burdened about his sins. No matter how hard he tried, (for he did try very hard) he often failed God. He knew God hated sin, that He could not excuse it, that it had to be punished. He knew that just trying to do right didn't wipe out all the bad things. And Daniel knew he could never make himself pure enough to enter God's holy Heaven.

So Daniel's heart leaped with joy when he understood that the Messiah would be cut off, destroyed, not for Himself, but for the sins of the people. The Messiah, who would come in a far-off, distant time, would pay for the sins Daniel could not pay for. The rest of the prophecy he could not understand, but that much he understood, and took, by faith.

For understanding about the rest of the prophecy, Daniel continued to pray. Many times a day, when he passed the open window of his apartment, which faced the west, where Jerusalem lay out across the desert, Daniel would drop to his knees in prayer.

Meanwhile, he was a faithful, loyal servant and advisor to King Darius. Because God was with him, everything Daniel did seemed to prosper. He was kind, but he was wise as well. King Darius found he could entrust his entire kingdom to Daniel. He announced his plans.

"We can't let the king give the kingdom to Daniel!" one prince complained.

"Right! We've got to stop Daniel!

"We deserve to be the king's advisers—not that Jew who prays all the time!"

"All right; let's stop him. But how?"

"We'll watch every move he makes. Surely he'll slip. We'll catch him making a mistake."

Daniel's enemies watched his every move with narrowed eyes, waiting to pounce on his first mistake. But Daniel didn't slip. God helped him to be wise.

"That guy never does wrong!" a prince pouted.

"No, never!" another agreed. "We may as well give up."

"Unless," another said ominously, "unless we can fix it so he has to break the king's law to keep one of the laws of his God. Why don't we get the king to pass a law that nobody prays except to him?" [42]

"Smart idea! We know Daniel won't stop praying. Then the king will have to punish him."

Daniel's enemies gathered into a tight knot and made their plans to trap Daniel. Poor, unsuspecting Daniel! Can they trap him?

12. The Plot Foiled

Why didn't someone warn King Darius? Why didn't they say, "Darius! Don't sign that decree! It's a wicked plot against Daniel's life!"? But no one did. When the princes approached King Darius on his golden throne in the palace of Babylon, they looked so sincere and honest, it didn't occur to the king to suspect them!

"Oh, King Darius," they said piously, "we are so glad you are our king. We want the whole world to know how important you are. We have a plan to honor you."

King Darius was pleased. After all, he was the conqueror of the mighty kingdom of Babylon. Yes, it would be nice to be honored by these princes.

"We have written up a decree," they added, "to show everyone your great power. This decree makes the rule that nobody can pray to any other man or god except you, for thirty days. If a man breaks this law, we have written that the punishment will be the den of lions." They all nodded to each other very wisely. "You don't have to do any of the work in making up

the law. We have it all written up here. All you need
to do is sign it. Make it a law of the Medes and
Persians, so it cannot be changed."

Now you'd think that a king with the power to
make a law that could not be changed, not ever, not by
anybody in the whole world, not even changed by the
king who made the law himself—you'd think that
king would be careful of what laws he made! But King
Darius was flattered. He liked the nice things these
men kept saying about him. He didn't even once think
what it might do to anyone else in the kingdom, least
of all his best friend and helper Daniel.

"I'll sign it," Darius said. And he did! It became
the law of the Medes and Persians that no one could
pray to any other man or god except Darius, for thirty
days.

"Now we've got him!" the princes whispered
greedily. "This is Daniel's death warrant. If he
doesn't pray, he isn't a good Jew. If he does pray, the
lions will eat him for supper tonight!"

As soon as Daniel heard about the decree, he went
to his own house. He fell to his knees beside his
chamber windows—just as he had done all the years
of his captivity. He faced the west, because that way,
in Jerusalem, was where God's holy temple had stood.

Years before, when King Solomon had built the
temple to God, he dedicated it with a prayer Daniel
had read again and again. King Solomon had knelt,

lifted up his hands to God, and prayed, "If your people sin, and You are angry with them and punish them by letting their enemies carry them off, if they are sorry for their sins, and pray to You facing this land and this house which I have built for You, then please dear God, hear their prayer, and forgive them." [43]

After Solomon built the temple, the children of Israel did sin. God did let their enemies carry them far off. That is why Daniel always prayed by his chamber windows, opened to the west, toward Jerusalem, toward the place where the temple had once stood.

The wicked princes knew exactly where to hide, to see if Daniel prayed. Sure enough, they caught Daniel praying! He hadn't hidden in a closet to pray. He prayed just as he always had! "Hurrah!" the princes shouted. "It's the lions' den for you, Daniel!"

Away they sped to tell the king. They were breathing hard, but they tried to act very solemn, as if they were terribly disappointed that someone had broken the king's command. "O King, didn't you sign a decree saying no one could pray to anyone except yourself?"

The king looked surprised. "Of course I did. You yourselves wrote up the law."

"Did it not forbid anyone to pray to anybody except you?"

"You know it did."

"Can you change the law now?"

"Certainly not. It is the law of the Medes and the Persians, and it cannot be changed."

"Oh, that's too bad, King. For we caught Daniel, that Jew, praying to his God. He paid absolutely no attention to the new law. Too bad. He'll just have to be thrown to the lions. That's the law, you know."

The king gasped. "Oh, no, not Daniel!" He had forgotten all about Daniel. "I forgot he always prays to his God. But I can't throw him into the lions' den!"

"You made the law."

"Well, I'll just have to find some way to alter the law," the king said, tight-lipped and angry with himself.

He went to the judges. "Please help me find a loophole so my friend Daniel won't have to be killed." Now the judges loved Darius and respected him, and they wanted to find a way to change the law. But they shook their heads.

He called his counsellors. "I have made a foolish law. Please help me to find a way to alter it."

They shook their heads. "There is no way to alter the laws of the Medes and Persians."

"The law cannot be broken."

He searched the old records for excuses or loopholes. He paced up and down in his royal chamber. All day long, he worked and worried, trying

(C) The Matson Photo Service, Alhambra, Calif 91803.

Basalt Lion marking Daniel's den of lions

to save Daniel. But it was no use. He couldn't find any way to change the law!

At sunset the princes came back. "Time's up, King Darius. Throw him to the lions."

It was true. There was nothing he could do. The law had to be kept. A land would soon turn to wickedness if the people found out the laws could be broken without any punishment. Tears sprang to the king's eyes. "Daniel, dear Daniel, I am so sorry. Please forgive me. I didn't realize what I was doing. But your God, the God you serve all the time, He will deliver you, won't He?"

Daniel looked at the king sorrowfully, and answered nothing.

The king motioned to the soldiers. They lifted the rock lid off the cave where the lions were kept. The lions leaped up at the men, snarling and slashing at them with their terrible claws. Hastily the soldiers lowered Daniel into the hole, then put the lid back on. The king sealed the rock so no one would try to come back and lift the lid off and rescue Daniel.

The king went back to his palace. He didn't want anybody around him. He sent the orchestra away. He didn't eat any supper. He couldn't sleep. All he could think about was the horrible pit where the lions were kept. He kept hearing their fierce growls, and the terrible smell of decaying human flesh. What would he find in the morning? Could Daniel's God truly keep him alive? Or would there be a small heap of bloody bones where the lions had gnawed them?

At dawn Darius hurried to the den, and had the stone lifted off. He called Daniel's name with a voice that broke with sorrow. "Daniel? Oh, Daniel, servant of the living God, is thy God whom you serve—is He able to deliver you from the lions?"

A strong, cheerful voice answered from the bottom of the pit. "Good morning, King Darius. Yes, my God sent His angel, to keep the lions' mouths shut. They couldn't hurt me. God knew I had done no wrong, King Darius."

Darius nodded sadly. "I know, Daniel, and I'm sorry." The king clapped his hands. "Bring ropes. Lift him out. Make haste!"

Back at the palace, King Darius called the princes to him. They came, and their mouths dropped open when they saw Daniel. Daniel alive? Daniel was alive!

"Tush!" a prince said. "The king must have fed the lions ahead of time. That's why they didn't eat Daniel. They weren't hungry. The king cheated."

"That's right," the princes all agreed. "The king must have cheated, and fed the lions so they weren't hungry for Daniel."

"You wicked men!" Darius shouted. "You've hated Daniel without a cause. Now you will find out if I fed the lions, or if God kept His servant Daniel."

The princes shrank back, and started screaming. "Soldiers, throw them to the lions!"

Before the bodies of those wicked men touched the bottom of the cave, the lions had torn them limb from limb! They found out, to their terror, that it was not that the lions were not hungry; it was that God had kept them from touching Daniel!

King Darius wrote another decree. This time it was a wise decree. "Men in every part of my great kingdom, tremble and fear the God of Daniel. He is the living God, and He will rule the world forever!"

13. Good News at Last

It seemed that the procession of kings would move on forever. Nebuchadnezzar, Evil-Merodach, Belteshazzar, Darius. . . .And now Cyrus had assumed the throne.[44] In the very first year of his reign, he issued a decree. Daniel could hardly believe his ears—it seemed too good to be true. But it was true. The Jews were going home at last. After seventy miserable years in captivity, the Jews were going back to Jerusalem. Cyrus, king of Persia, had decreed it himself.

"The Lord God of heaven hath given me all the kingdoms of the earth," the decree began, "and he hath charged me to build him a house at Jerusalem. Who is there among you of all his people? His God be with him, and let him go up to Jerusalem, and build the house of the Lord God of Israel (he is *the* God) which is in Jerusalem." [45]

Daniel read the decree, and lifted his face toward Heaven. The tears trickled down his wrinkled cheeks on to his gray beard. "Thank you, thank you, dear

Heavenly Father," he whispered, "for forgiving our sins and taking us home."

Daniel's mind leaped back to the promises God had made long ago. Isaiah wrote that Cyrus would rebuild the temple, long before Nebuchadnezzar had destroyed it. It was a miracle, and it was happening before his eyes!

Daniel remembered the prophecy of the weeping prophet Jeremiah. He was dead now, too, but he had written, before it all happened, that Nebuchadnezzar would capture Jerusalem, and that the people would be captives in Babylon for 70 years. And that was exactly how long it had been since the terrible day Daniel had ridden through the desert sands with Ashpenaz toward Babylon. Oh, how good God was to keep His Word exactly!

The caravan assembled for the three-month trip back. But it was different now, from when the Jews came to Babylon. Then they were in rags, starved with hunger, slaves, their king blinded and in chains, his sons slain. But now, going home, the Jews were leaving with their camels and asses loaded down with good things: food piled high, gold and silver, extra animals, a letter from the king commanding any needs they had be supplied by the governors, and most important, the precious gold vessels from the House of God.[40] Their hearts were so full of praise, they sang a psalm together again and again: "When the Lord turned again the captivity of Zion, we were like them that dream. Then was our mouth filled with laughter, and our tongue with singing: then said they among the heathen, The Lord hath done great things for them. The Lord *hath* done great things for us; whereof we are glad."[47]

King Cyrus appointed prince Zerubbabel to lead the expedition.[48] Zerubbabel had been born in Babylon.[49] He was one of King Jehoiachin's grandsons.[50] Jehoiachin had been such a wicked man that God had cursed him, and said no child of his could ever be king of Judah.[51] Zerubbabel would never be king—but he didn't even think about that. He could still serve God, and he did, with all his heart.

Messengers from Jerusalem came back to Daniel and told him all about Zerubbabel's work. The first job he started was to rebuild the great temple of God. He took a plumbline, and a level to make sure the foundations were exactly level. Then he measured off the distances. People laughed, seeing Zerubbabel standing on the rubble of the old temple, marking with a ball of string where the new foundations would go. But God sent a prophet (God always has a prophet to tell people what is right), the prophet Zechariah, who said, "Don't despise the day of small things. God is going to help Zerubbabel build this temple."[52]

And God did help him. Two years later, the

foundations of the new temple were laid, and ready to dedicate. The joyful people met together, to praise the Lord. But some of the old men, who remembered the first temple which Solomon had built, wept. They remembered how magnificent it was, how marvellous the beauty of its gold-panelled walls, and they saw how plain and unornamented this one would be. The sounds of their weeping mixed with the sounds of joy and laughter, so it was hard to tell which it was.[53]

All this was told to Daniel by messengers from Jerusalem. And he laughed and wept as he listened, but mostly wept. For Daniel was now about ninety years old. He did not get to go back home from Babylon. King Cyrus had insisted he stay and help him. Daniel served him faithfully, just as he had served the kings of Babylon through the seventy years of captivity. Daniel wanted to be where God wanted him to be. But still, he couldn't help weeping when he heard the news of the temple. That was his home. Those were his people. He longed to see again the green hills of Judea.

"Dear Lord," he prayed, "I'm so tired. When can I go home? How much longer must I wait?"

While Daniel wept and prayed and fasted because of his sorrow, up in Heaven an angel was waiting impatiently. He had a message from God for Daniel, and he could hardly wait to give it to him. It was so

important, so wonderful, he could hardly stand still
until it was the time God had set for him to go!

14. Broken Brick Walls and Stars

The news which the next messenger brought from Jerusalem was discouraging. Daniel's heart sank as he listened.

"They got the foundation of the temple laid, Daniel. It was a beautiful sight!—with the priests dressed in their garments of white and blue, and the trumpets and cymbals playing, and all the people singing. I wish you could have seen it."

Daniel nodded quietly. Not a muscle in his face betrayed the disappointment he had felt because he'd prayed for that for seventy years, and then didn't get to see it. But he had talked it over with the Lord, and the Lord had said plainly, "No, Daniel, not yet." So Daniel smiled at the messenger and said, only, "Yes, it must have been wonderful."

"But there's trouble now, Daniel."

"What kind of trouble?"

"Well, you remember the kind of people Nebuchadnezzar left in Jerusalem—just the poorest kind of folks. They've been causing trouble ever since the captives got back."

"How is that?"

"They keep threatening Zerubbabel and Jeshua. They've scared off everybody, so nobody is working on the temple right now. And it's too big a job for Zerubbabel to do by himself, though he keeps trying."

Daniel's voice was sharp. "You mean nobody is working on the temple?"

"No, sir. See, these men who lived there, they keep talking very piously about how they'd like to help, and how much they love God, and how they are really causing all this trouble just because they want to do it right."[54]

"*Nobody* working on the temple?" Daniel interrupted.

"No, sir."

Daniel was grieved. His people had finally gotten back home. But they were not yet worshipping God in His own temple. Would they never find rest?

For three weeks Daniel wept and mourned. Food didn't taste good. He didn't think about the beautiful clothes he owned. He did nothing but weep and pray, and confess his sins and the sins of all the Jews.

Finally, God up in Heaven smiled, and told the angel he could leave with his message!

One day, Daniel stood on the banks of the Tigris River with his friends.[55] He looked up and saw—what was it? *Who* was it? It was a Man, a Man whose body shone like lamps of fire. His feet glistened like polished brass. Daniel's friends could see nothing, but a terrible fear gripped them, and they ran away.

Daniel looked at the vision, and his knees buckled under him. He felt so unworthy! He fell down flat on the ground and hid his face in shame. For this was not a man, not an angel, but God's Son Himself!

An angel touched Daniel on the shoulder—it was the angel who had waited so impatiently for permission to deliver his message—and lifted Daniel to his hands and knees. "Daniel, God loves you dearly. Please stand up on your feet, for I have a message from Him for you."

Daniel stood up, but his legs were trembling.

"Don't be afraid. From that first day, three weeks ago, when you made up your mind to confess your sins, and find out what God wanted through all this, God heard your prayers. He sent me to come to you, but one of Satan's demons stopped me. Michael, one of God's chief angels, came to help me get to you. God has sent me to tell you what is going to happen to your people, the Jews. It won't happen for a long time yet."

Daniel could hear the angel's words, but he couldn't make his mouth move to answer him, because he was so scared. Then Jesus, the One whom Daniel had seen at the first, the One with the face like lightning, bent over and touched his lips.

Then Daniel stammered, "How can I, your servant, talk to You when You are so holy?"

"O man greatly beloved, don't be afraid," Jesus said quietly. "Peace be unto you. Be strong, yes, be strong."

"Speak, dear Lord," Daniel said humbly, "for you have made me strong."

Jesus began to tell Daniel many, many things that will happen some day—wars that will be fought, terrible sins wicked men will commit, the awful persecution the Jews will suffer. Daniel listened, amazed.[56] Then he wrote down every word the Lord spoke.

"One day, dear Daniel, your people will be delivered. I promise you that every one whose name is written in the book of life will be delivered. Many of them that sleep in the dust of the earth shall awake, some to everlasting life, and some to shame and everlasting contempt. Those that be wise will shine like the brightness of heaven, and they that turn many to righteousness will shine like the stars for ever and ever." [57]

But it was all too much. Daniel couldn't understand it all. "O my Lord, what shall be the end of these things?"

"Some day you will understand," Jesus answered kindly, "but not now. Close the book, Daniel. Put down your pen. Write no more. Seal the book until the end comes.''

Daniel obeyed numbly.

"Daniel, you have been a good servant. When you were but a youth, and carried captive far from your home and family, you did right. During the seventy-three years since, you have been faithful. The threat of the king's sword and the lions' den did not stop you from serving Me. Now you may rest. One great day, I will reward you for your lifetime of faithfulness.''

.   .   .   .

In the burning desert sands of Arabia, not far from the fabled city of Bagdad, looms an enormous broad mount near the palm-lined banks of the Euphrates River. For years it puzzled travellers. Why was it flat-topped? Why was there just one such mount on the broad plain? About seventy years ago a man named Koldeway started digging down into the mysterious mountain. He dug far, far down into the packed soil, and there he found—Babylon! Babylon, in ruins. They were all there—the great Ishtar gate with its dragons and griffons on the walls; the vast Processional Way, decorated with a hundred stone lions baring their teeth; the high broad walls and towers, with flecks of blue enamel still clinging to them; the huge temple which Nebuchadnezzar had built to Merodach—they were all there, but they were ruins, ruins, broken heaps of brick and rubble.

The words of the prophet Isaiah had come true: "And Babylon, the glory of kingdoms, the beauty of the Chaldees' excellency, shall be as when God overthrew Sodom and Gomorrah. It shall never be inhabited, neither shall it be dwelt in from generation to generation: neither shall the Arabian pitch tent there; neither shall the shepherds make their fold there. But wild beasts of the desert shall lie there; and their houses shall be full of doleful creatures; and owls shall dwell there and satyrs shall dance there. And the wild beasts of the islands shall cry in their desolate houses, and dragons in their pleasant palaces." [58]

Yes, Babylon is in ruins. For hundreds of years, the drifting, shifting sands covered it, so that men forgot where it stood. Covered were the ruined walls, the temples, the gardens. And covered again by the sands they may be, and men may once again forget where mighty Babylon stood.

But Daniel—dear, faithful, brave Daniel, who served the Lord throughout a lifetime of terrible trial—Daniel will live forever. The man who served many kings because he loved God, will forever serve The King of Heaven and earth, God Himself. Because he was wise, and turned many to righteousness, he will shine as the stars forever and ever.

Scripture References

1 Jer. 46:22-26
2 Jer. 6:22, 23
3 Judg. 7:22
4 Jer. 32: 35
5 II Kings 23:37; 24:4
6 II Kings 24:7
7 Jer. 27:8
8 Dan. 1:2
9 Jer. 25:1-11
10 Jer. 26:20-23
11 Dan. 1:3-20
12 Lev. 11 & 17
13 Dan. 2
14 Gen. 10:8-10
15 Gen. 11:2-9
16 Dan. 2:24
17 Jer. 36:22-24
18 II Kings 24:1-5;
    II Chron. 36:5-8;
    Jer. 22:18, 19
19 II Kings 24:6-16;
    II Chron. 36: 9, 10
20 Jer. 29:1-10
21 Jer. 38:6-9

22 Ezek. 2:1-7
23 II Kings 25:1-21;
    II Chron. 36:11-21
24 Dan. 3
26 Isa. 46:1, 2; Jer. 48:7
27 Dan. 4
28 Ezek. 21:19-22
29 II Kings 25:27-30;
    Jer. 52:31-34
30 Dan. 7
31 Early years of Cyrus
    told in Herodotus,
    Book I, 107-125
32 Dan. 8:4, 20
33 Isa. 44:28; 45:1-4
34 Isa. 13:17-22
35 Herodotus, Book I, 191
36 Daniel 5
37 Dan. 6:1-3
38 Jer. 29:10
39 Dan. 9:25, 26
40 Gen. 3:15
41 Deut. 18:15, 18
42 Dan. 6

43 II Chron. 6:36-39

44 Dan. 10:1

45 Ezra 1:1-3

46 Ezra 1:5-11

47 Psalm 126:1-3

48 Ezra 2:2; 3:8

49 "Zerubbabel" means "born in Babylon"

50 I Chron. 3:16-19

51 Jer. 22:24-30; I Chron. 3:16 (Jeconiah is the same as Jehoiachin and Coniah)

52 Zech. 4:6-10

53 Ezra 3:8-13

54 Ezra 4:1-5

55 Daniel 10

56 Daniel 11

57 Daniel 12:2, 3

58 Isaiah 13:19-22

Chronology of Book of Daniel

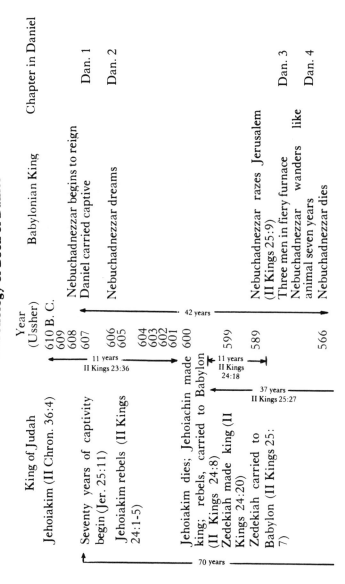

King of Judah	Year (Ussher)	Babylonian King	Chapter in Daniel
Jehoiakim (II Chron. 36:4)	610 B. C. 609 608 607	Nebuchadnezzar begins to reign Daniel carried captive	Dan. 1
Seventy years of captivity begin (Jer. 25:11)	606 605	Nebuchadnezzar dreams	Dan. 2
Jehoiakim rebels (II Kings 24:1-5)	604 603 602 601		
Jehoiakim dies; Jehoiachin made king; rebels, carried to Babylon (II Kings 24:8) Zedekiah made king (II Kings 24:20)	600 599		
Zedekiah carried to Babylon (II Kings 25:7)	589	Nebuchadnezzar razes Jerusalem (II Kings 25:9) Three men in fiery furnace	Dan. 3
	566	Nebuchadnezzar wanders like animal seven years Nebuchadnezzar dies	Dan. 4

11 years — II Kings 23:36

42 years

11 years II Kings 24:18

37 years — II Kings 25:27

70 years

Date	Event	Reference
563	Evil-Merodach begins to reign	(II Kings 25:27)
557	Belshazzar begins to reign	Dan. 7
556		
555	Daniel's vision of ram and goat	Dan. 8
538	Belshazzar sees writing on wall; slain	Dan. 5
537	Darius begins to reign	Dan. 6
536	Cyrus conquers Babylon; decrees rebuilding of temple (Ezra 1:3)	Dan. 9
535		
534	Daniel's vision of glory of God	Dan. 10, 11, 12

├── 20 years ──┤ ├─ 3 years ─┤ Dan. 10:1

Jehoiachin's captivity ended

Seventy years of captivity end

For a complete list of books available from the Sword of the Lord, write to Sword of the Lord Publishers, P. O. Box 1099, Murfreesboro, Tennessee 37133.